P9-CQG-695

DAN YACCARINO

BILLY AND GOAT AT THE STATE FAIR

ALFRED A. KNOPF NEW YORK

Billy and Goat were
the best of friends.

Billy liked to swing,
and Goat liked to push.

Billy stuck to the path,
but Goat made his own way.

Billy liked to fix the tractor, and Goat liked to ride it.

Billy liked to smell the flowers,
and Goat liked to eat them!

Together, they made a great pair.

Billy liked reading adventure stories,

but Goat was always looking for *real-life* adventures. . . .

VISIT THE
STATE
RIDES!
CORN
DOGS!
BEST-GOAT
COMPETITION!

And he found one! The big state fair was coming!

There was even a best-goat competition. Billy could tell that Goat really wanted to go. And why not? Billy already knew who the best goat was.

So Billy washed
Goat's fur . . .

. . . and scrubbed his
hooves till they shined.

When the day of the fair
arrived, Billy was sure
Goat would be awarded
the blue ribbon.

The state fair was huge! And loud! And full of people! There were so many things to see and do and eat. Goat was excited!

But Billy was scared. The state fair was huge! And loud! And full of people! Still, he really wanted Goat to win. He'd have to be brave.

Billy and Goat made their way through the crowds, past rides and games and displays,

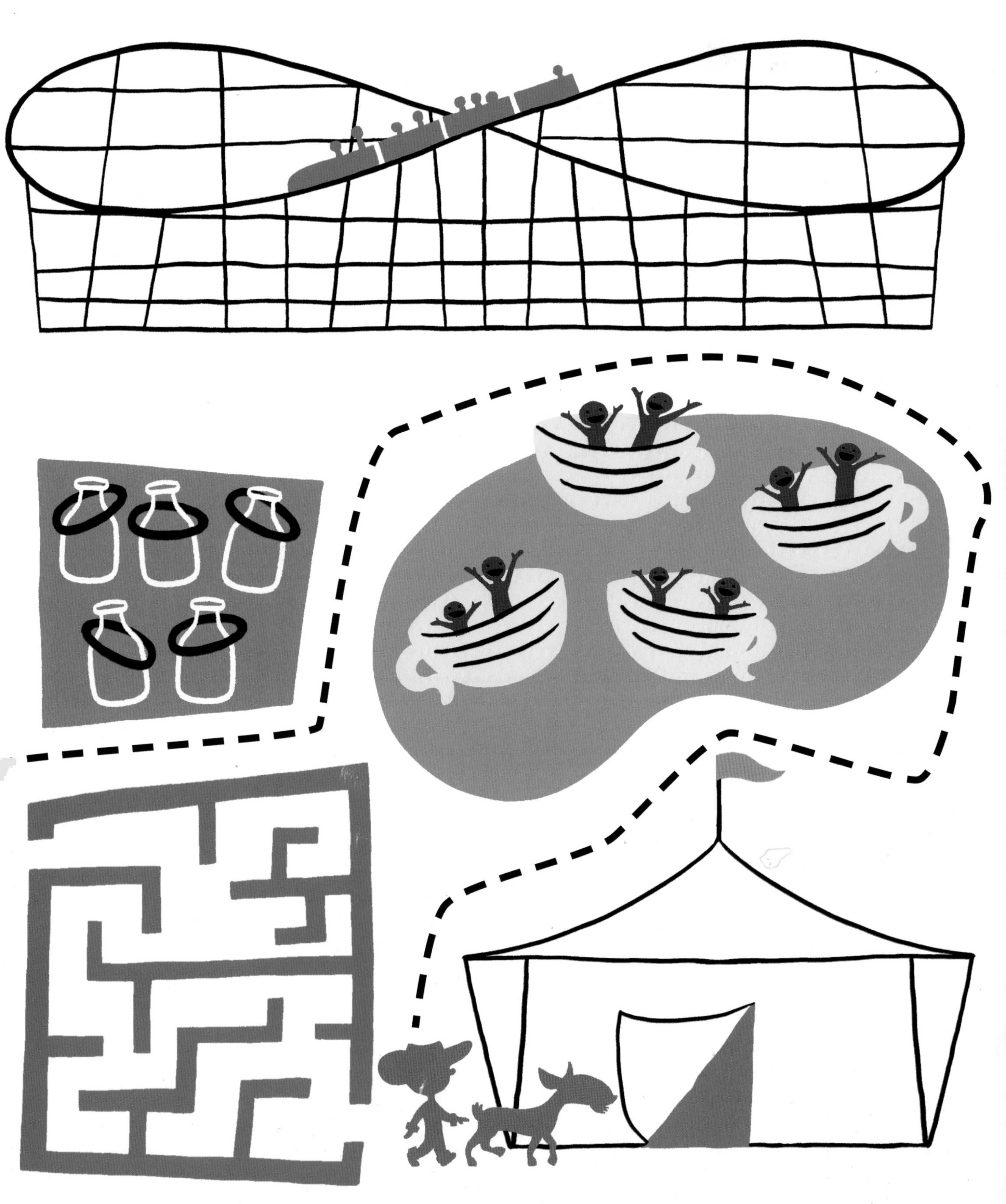

and–*phew!*–finally found the livestock tent.

It was nice and quiet inside, and Billy was happy to wait in the tent for the competition to begin. . . .

But not Goat!
He wanted an adventure!

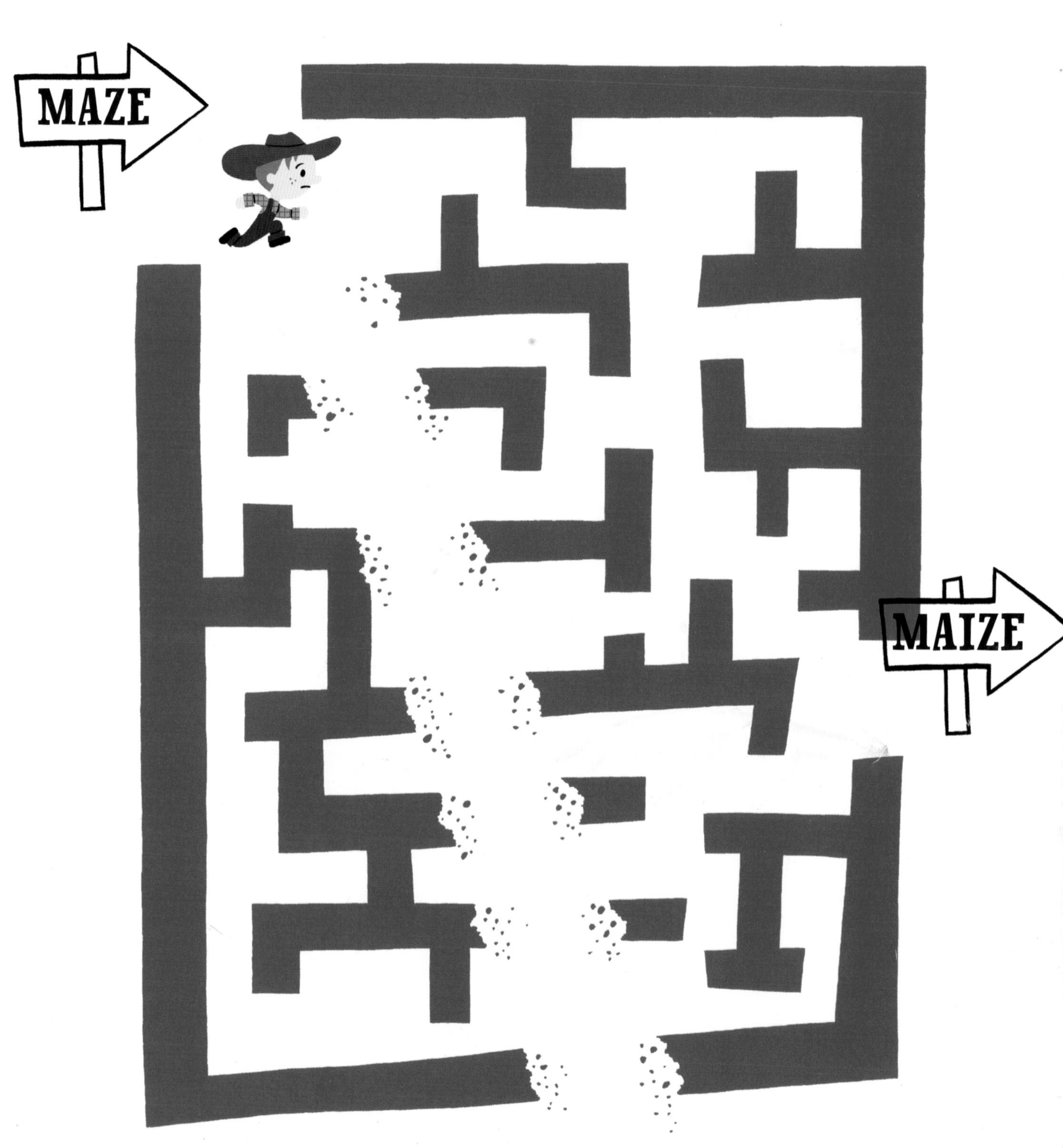

The maze looked like fun to Goat, and was easy to get through once he made a shortcut.

Goat loved the log plunge.

There were so many things to see.

To ride.

To hear.

And to eat!

Billy's heart was racing when he finally caught up with Goat.

"I was afraid you'd get lost!" he panted. "I was afraid *I'd* get lost!" Then Billy looked around and realized where they were sitting.

They were on the biggest float in the parade! The crowd roared and the band played—and everything was just plain BIG. But with Goat by his side, Billy decided it was also actually . . . *fun!*

For the rest of the day, Billy and Goat explored the fair—together.

They rode every ride.

They came in third (and fourth) in the pie-eating contest.

They joined the yodeling competition.

And enjoyed the floral displays.

They shared corn dogs. (Goat thought the sticks were delicious.)

Billy loved the teacup ride best.

Goat's favorite was the roller coaster!

Finally, they headed back to the livestock tent—just in time to see the blue ribbon awarded to . . . *another* goat.

But neither of them minded. They'd had an amazing adventure at the fair. Besides Billy already knew who the best goat *really* was.

For Robbie

THIS IS A BORZOI BOOK PUBLISHED BY ALFRED A. KNOPF

 Published in the United States by Alfred A. Knopf, an imprint of Random House Children's Books, a division of Random House LLC, a Penguin Random House Company, New York.

Knopf, Borzoi Books, and the colophon are registered trademarks of Random House LLC.

Visit us on the Web! randomhousekids.com

Educators and librarians, for a variety of teaching tools, visit us at RHTeachersLibrarians.com

Library of Congress Cataloging-in-Publication Data

Yaccarino, Dan, author, illustrator.

Billy & Goat at the state fair / Dan Yaccarino. – First edition.

p. cm.

Summary: A visit to the state fair cements the friendship between a boy and a goat who are very different from one another.

ISBN 978-0-385-75325-8 (trade) – ISBN 978-0-385-75326-5 (lib. bdg.) – ISBN 978-0-385-75327-2 (ebook)

[1. Friendship–Fiction. 2. Goats–Fiction. 3. Fairs–Fiction.] I. Title. II. Title: Billy and Goat at the state fair.

PZ7.Y125Bjh 2015 [E]–dc23 2014038461

The illustrations in this book were created with brush and ink on vellum and Adobe Photoshop.

MANUFACTURED IN MALAYSIA

August 2015 10 9 8 7 6 5 4 3 2 1 First Edition